T0287874

MORE PRAISE FOR

BEFORE THE DARK COMES

"Arturo Mantecón has translated some of the most complex Spanish-language poets, which is to say, he has spent years imitating the inimitable, wearing the language of masters, sharpening his instincts for literary play and deception. José Primitivo Charlevoix's *Before the Dark Comes*, like the work of every great heteronym, represents the author's quest to know the furthest reaches of himself."

Maceo Montoya
educator, artist, author of *Preparatory Notes for Future Masterpieces*

"*Before the Dark Comes* is a feast of pan-color, kneadable language—love dissected into guttural atoms of the extreme, a private, visceral truth utterly stripped of the trite gaudiness of confessional poetry. José Primitivo Charlevoix, the enigmatic Salvador Dalí of words—I would nail each of these poems onto a wall, yet neither above my bed or in my living-room, not even in a picture gallery—each of the pieces is as huge in its impact as a mural."

Svetlana Lavochkina
Ukrainian-born novelist, poet, and translator

"These poems are in search of an author. Sometimes they ascribe a certain identity to themselves; other times they disclose their adherence to something that can only be found beyond our ability to perceive, something that sends a chill down the reader's spine: 'all of my bones / whistle to the hungering wind.' At times, they display surreal, dreamy qualities: 'the man stands upon a milking stool,' or 'hammurabi came to me / with the morning star / in the skittering light / of the sinning moon.' Under one cover, they appear as a formidable body of work that any lover of intuitive poetry should have on his book-shelf."

Anatoly Kudryavitsky
Russian-Irish novelist, poet, editor, and literary translator

NOMADIC PRESS

OAKLAND

PHILADELPHIA

BROOKLYN

WWW.NOMADICPRESS.ORG

MASTHEAD
FOUNDING PUBLISHER
J. K. Fowler

ASSOCIATE EDITOR
Michaela S. Mullin

EDITOR
Noelia Cerna

DESIGN
Jevohn Tyler Newsome

MISSON STATEMENT Through publications, events, and active community participation, Nomadic Press collectively weaves together platforms for intentionally marginalized voices to take their rightful place within the world of the written and spoken word. Through our limited means, we are simply attempting to help right the centuries' old violence and silencing that should never have occurred in the first place and build alliances and community partnerships with others who share a collective vision for a future far better than today.

INVITATIONS Nomadic Press wholeheartedly accepts invitations to read your work during our open reading period every year. To learn more or to extend an invitation, please visit: www.nomadicpress.org/invitations

DISTRIBUTION
Orders by teachers, libraries, trade bookstores, or wholesalers:

Nomadic Press Distribution
orders@nomadicpress.org
(510) 500-5162

Small Press Distribution
spd@spdbooks.org
(510) 524-1668 / (800) 869-7553

This book was made possible by a loving community of chosen family and friends, old and new.

For author questions or to book a reading at your bookstore, university/school, or alternative establishment, please send an email to info@nomadicpress.org.

Cover art: "Houston Toad" by Lisa Studier

Published by Nomadic Press, 111 Fairmount Avenue, Oakland, California 94611

First printing, 2022

Library of Congress Cataloging-in-Publication Data

Title: *Before the Dark Comes*
p. cm.
Summary: Arturo Mantecón, translator and bibliophile, chances upon a strange leather-bound book found in a vast private library. Chaotic poetry. Grotesque images. But who, exactly, is the author? Is it José Primitivo Charlevoix, or someone else? Mantecón searches for clues within the curious text itself, and the clues he finds lead him to the unlikely locations of Quebec and Ontario.

[1. POETRY / American / Hispanic & Latino. 2. POETRY / Subjects & Themes / Love. 3. POETRY / Subjects & Themes / Death, Grief, Loss. 4. POETRY / American / General.] I. III. Title.

LIBRARY OF CONGRESS CONTROL NUMBER: 2021951087

ISBN: 978-1-955239-25-7

BEFORE THE DARK COMES

JOSÉ PRIMITIVO CHARLEVOIX

EDITED BY ARTURO MANTECÓN

BEFORE THE DARK COMES

JOSÉ PRIMITIVO CHARLEVOIX

EDITED BY ARTURO MANTECÓN

**NOMADIC
PRESS**

FOR MY LOVE,
CLIONA

CONTENTS

foreword
by Ivan Argüelles

editor's note
Shadow Hunt: The Search for José Primitivo Charlevoix

jpm	1
and who will bother	3
[my cliona is]	5
96857	8
simple	13
quand un telescope est hors de question	16
abysmal beautiful face	18
the dragon and the boar	21
my lady of the trolleys	25
sensibilia	30
cliona and the giant in the lake	33
cliona wanted an egg	38
[my cliona descended]	43
[hammurabi came to me]	45
the electric car	51
black mountain	54
the toad	58
what cliona did with the head of god	89

reading guide

FOREWORD

It is no accident that Arturo Mantecón's introduction to *Before the Dark Comes* opens with the following epigraph:

> *Não sou ninguém, ninguém...*
> *Sou uma figura de romance*
> *por escrever, passando aérea*
> *e desfeita sem ter sido,*
> *entre os sonhos de quem*
> *me não soube completer*
> Bernardo Soares
> *Livro do Desassossego*

This quote is from Fernando Pessoa's *Book of Disquiet*, written under the pseudonym Bernardo Soares, one of the many personae employed by Pessoa. One suspects that the persona of José Primitivo Charlevoix belongs to someone else as well, as there is something of the literary hoax in the "biographical" preface to the work. I am inclined to assign the authorship of this text to Sacramento poet Arturo Mantecón, who is no stranger to this type of literature. Mantecón has recently translated and published a selection by Mexican poet Mario Santiago Papasquiaro (*Poetry Come out of My Mouth*, 2018). Santiago Papasquiaro (actually the name of a city in the state of Durango, Mexico), who died tragically in 1998, is the pseudonym of José Alfredo Zendejas Pineda, co-founder with Roberto Bolaño of the Infrarrealista school of poetry.

Papasquiaro appears as the character Ulises Lima in Bolaño's cele-
brated novel Los Detectives salvajes, the fundamental plot of which is
the hunting down of an apocryphal Mexican poet. With this in mind,
the long quasi-fictitious prose preface to this book puts us in the familiar
territory of literary hoax: the supposed editor of this work discovers this
manuscript in a San Francisco Victorian mansion and after many a twist
and turn identifies the "author" as a French-Canadian, José Primitivo
Charlevoix. This piece has the feel of Borges, another writer given to the
tradition of the hoax.

The poems in *Before the Dark Comes* are distinctly modernist,
demented at times, hallucinatory and obsessive; with a self-defined
comparison to Lautréamont, they also have some affinity to the surre-
alism of Breton and Lamantia. The book is dedicated to a fictive woman,
"my Cliona," and many of the poems are for or about her:

> *my cliona is my hatred*
> *my tethered wolf*
> *my red sea urchin*
> *my misshapen pearl*
> *my cliona is my love ...*
> *my nest of yellow ants*

Despite the surrealistic modernity of these poems, there are distinct
elements of the archaic (going back to Gilgamesh) or of the fantastic
medieval (like Malory), and exemplary of these qualities is the poem
"[hammurabi came to me]" with its allusions that hearken back to Sumer
and Akkad. Of particular note is a long poem, largely a prose poem, "The
Toad," in which each of the sections end with the same haunting refrain: "a
poison toad beckoning to me with eyes empty and alldevouring," a repet-
itive technique that reminds one of Poe. The overall effect of these poems
is that of a mind haunted and maddened in a landscape at times of bleak

post-modernity, with titles such as "96847" or "abysmal beautiful face." The strange almost fey lyricism of this work is somewhat rare nowadays and bears some comparison with Olchar Lindsann's *Arthur dies*. Whoever the author of these poems may be, the book is exciting and experimental and stands out in contrast to the plethora of self-confessional, thinly disguised prose that passes for poetry nowadays.

Charlevoix is quite clearly a descendant of the Infrarrealistas!

Ivan Argüelles
author of *Immobility* (2022)

EDITOR'S NOTE

Shadow Hunt: The Search for José Primitivo Charlevoix

> *No tienen los sapos nombre*
> *cuando mueren en el monte*
>> Leopoldo María Panero
>> "Resurrección de la Carne"

> *Não sou ninguém, ninguém...*
> *Sou uma figura de romance*
> *por escrever, pasando aérea*
> *e desfeita sem ter sido,*
> *entre os sonhos de quem*
> *me não soube completer*
>> Bernardo Soares
>> *Livro do Desassossego*

My friend and publisher of my translations of Leopoldo María Panero's poetry (*Like an eye in the hand of a beggar*), Dennis Letbetter, is a wonderful photographer, an eccentric interior decorator, and a relentless accumulator of books. Some six years ago, circumstances required that he sell a great part of his collection, a collection that lay in shelves and in numerous yard-high stacks on the floors of his three-story Victorian mansion on Masonic Avenue in San Francisco.

I visited him during this period and offered to buy some books from his collection. He refused to sell me any, giving some convoluted excuse that I did not have the energy to dispute. He instead said that I could browse the bookshelves on the top floor of his house and pick any book I wanted, but one book, and one only.

I climbed the stairs, the sound of a siren screaming down sordid and busy Haight Street growing fainter the higher I climbed. When I reached the top level of the stairs, I had to brush aside juniper and angle through cattails that Dennis had arranged there along with a broad bed of stones, all to give the feel of being beside a river. I stepped carefully, yet I still twisted my ankle on the smooth river rock.

At last I stood unsteady before a series of shelves going all the way up to the ceiling, painted sky-blue and daubed and sponged depictions of white cirrus clouds.

Any book I wanted...but there were hundreds and hundreds of them in a universe collapsing back into itself in swift blue shift—and I abandoned any thought of examining every volume in the oaken racks. Without a step stool or other prop, I hadn't a prayer of reading even the mere spines in the topmost shelves of the nine-foot bookcases, and the cumbersome river rock—some stones as round as and twice the breadth of a Pugliese loaf—would require manual excavation in order to provide a level surface for the legs of a stool.

And so, confronted with a sheer cliff of books, I spent a couple of hours focusing on the volumes at eye level—and finally selected an intriguing title on a shelf of the middle oak bookcase: *Before the Dark Comes* by José Primitivo Charlevoix.

Bound in what appeared to be red Moroccan leather, the book bore no publisher's name, no printer's name, and no date—though it seemed contemporary. It consisted of 51 pages of mixed prose and poetry that I would characterize as extremely strange—decidedly interesting, but rather raw and wildly careless. There were no illustrations. The font looked something like Courier. The title page included a dedication: "FOR MY LOVE CLIONA."

When I returned to my friend with the book in hand, he confessed that he could tell me nothing about it—in fact, he was unaware of its existence—but figured it may very well have been accidentally included in a larger lot of books purchased at some eccentric bookstore—perhaps in Toronto, perhaps in Manhattan or London...he really could not venture a better guess at its origin.

A thorough internet search on my part turned up nothing for the author or the title.

After reading the book for the third time, I decided that José Primitivo Charlevoix was comparable in his outrageous style to le Comte de Lautréamont, the author of *Les Chants de Maldoror*.

Before the Dark Comes is animated by a not-at-all-quaint blasphemousness. Cliona, the terrible mistress of the narrator, is at war with the biblical god, and the book abounds in dragons, encounters with freakish prophets, and monstrous, gnostic toads.

Charlevoix has certain lexical and syntactical idiosyncrasies more commonly associated with some modern poets. He employs no capitalization. He eschews all punctuation, including apostrophes. Words that are normally hyphenated are put together as compounds. Other words are strung together without spacing, but this reader cannot surmise to what intended effect. On the other hand, he employs line breaks and indentations in various places, particularly in the poems that are broken out into irregular stanzas, apparently for emphasis.

I was intrigued, and I decided to do all I could to republish the book, but not without first attempting to find out who José Primitivo Charlevoix was. For all I knew, he was alive. For all I knew, some publisher or family member or executor held the rights to his work.

So I set myself to search for clues in the words of the book as to the identity and origin of Charlevoix.

I came to a quick conclusion that the poet was not from the United States. The text of the book contains several examples of non-US orthography: "neighbour" and "colour" and "meagre" and "lustre." These spellings are most common in Great Britain, Canada, and Australia. I am less certain about the spelling habits of the anglophone inhabitants of India and Pakistan.

One of the pieces in the book makes mention of black squirrels. I am familiar with these squirrels that form a melanistic subgroup of the eastern gray squirrel, having grown up in Michigan where they are quite common. I had also spotted them the couple of times I had visited Niagara Falls and Toronto. Research indicated that their range was concentrated in Eastern Canada, Michigan and parts of Northern Ohio. I assumed that the author was no Michigander and began to search for other clues that might point to a Canadian origin for him. First, there was the French surname, Charlevoix—rather incongruous coupled with his two forenames but a possible indicator, nonetheless.

I then scoured the poems and prose for possible objects, landmarks or place names that would have a Canadian flavor, and I came upon a reference to Fossambault. Fossambault-sur-le-Lac is a small town (presently with some 1,700 inhabitants) near Lake Saint-Joseph and approximately 10 miles to the northeast of Quebec City in Canada.

Proceeding on a hunch, I made phone calls to several vital statistics agencies in Quebec, until finally hitting upon the right one: the office of le Directeur de l'état civil in Sainte-Foy.

Monsieur Gérard Kérouac (yes, Kérouac) informed me that there were no records for a José Primitivo Charlevoix—but that there was an adoption record for a *Joseph-Primitif Charlevoix*. I asked for details and was told that it was not possible to obtain this information over the phone; if I were serious about this matter, I could come to the offices of l'état civil and would be shown the document after presenting satisfactory proof of my identification and filling out an affidavit stating that I was doing genealogical/biographical research.

I was living in Traverse City, Michigan at the time, and the trip by car to Sainte-Foy was not difficult or too time-consuming.

Gérard Kérouac was gracious and amiable and, upon my telling him that I was a poet, invited me to dinner at Chez Rioux, a wonderful restaurant where I dined on tartare de cerf rouge. I was excited by the morning discoveries, and the conversation was delightful. My new friend revealed that he was related to the poet Émile Nelligan on his mother's side. We spoke through cheese and fruit, parfaits that were perfect, and demitasses for several hours, and we parted on a promise to meet again in Northern Michigan—but I digress...

The file that he opened that morning contained a certificate of adoption (dated June 16, 1935) of one Joseph-Primitif Charlevoix, approximately 6 months old. The adopting party whose signature appeared at the foot of the page was François-Xavier Charlevoix (Célibataire), resident of Fossambault-sur-le-Lac, 37 years of age, occupation as deacon of Sainte-Catherine church in the town of Sainte-Catherine-de-la-Jacques-Cartier.

In the same file was another certificate of adoption, in Spanish and signed May 31, 1935, with flourishes by Monseñor Emilio Morales Roque, presiding pastor of the Cathedral San Miguel Arcángel and Apostolic Administrator of the Archbishopric of Tegucigalpa, Honduras. The document stated that Francisco Xavier Charlevoix (canadiense) was, by means of the signed instrument, granted adoption and custody of a male child foundling, date of birth unknown, parents unknown, baptized May 22 with the names José Primitivo Morales (He was given the surname of the church pastor.). Witnesses were Father Mario Santos Mesa and Father

Sarapio Saltillo Molina.

So now I knew much more about my poet than before, and though I had determined that he was a Honduran foundling, perhaps an orphan, adopted by a Quebecois cleric in 1935, these revelations seemed to point to greater unknowns.

Two days later, I traveled to Sainte-Catherine's, the parish church of Sainte-Catherine-de-la-Jacques-Cartier and Fossambault-sur-le-Lac, and I spoke to Father Jean-Paul Hébert de Saint-Denys.

He had told me, the previous day over the phone, that indeed there had been a church deacon by the name of François-Xavier Charlevoix. There was little about him in the church records other than his ordination in 1922 and the extent of his years of service, but he was a man of extraordinary kindness who was remembered by many who lived near the shores of Lake Saint-Joseph. Father Jean-Paul would be happy, he said, to tell me what he knew—and he knew a great deal.

Jean-Paul said that he was but a boy when Deacon Charlevoix returned to Fossambault after a long absence, but his father was a friend of the deacon's and spoke of him often. His father had told him that Charlevoix was a good man but given over to prolonged spells of sadness which almost always precipitated long bouts of drinking.

His formal studies had been in theology and church doctrine, but he was an avid amateur entomologist. In the mid-1930s, he took advantage of a clerical exchange program between Quebec and the missionary territories of Central America and went to Honduras. His hidden purpose was to study lepidoptera in a nearby rainforest; but instead of returning with boxes of mounted specimens of butterflies and moths, he came home with an infant boy.

He was very secretive about the baby, and only his aging mother, who took care of the boy when François-Xavier was away at the church, spent any time with him.

When the boy reached school age, François-Xavier declined to enroll him in the parish school and home-schooled him.

After his mother died, François-Xavier's drunken benders became worse and more frequent, until the parish priest told him he could no longer be deacon. This was sometime around 1947 or '48, and shortly thereafter, François-Xavier bade Jean-Paul's father adieu, saying that a cousin had found work for him in a paper mill in Kitchener.

The assumption was he took the boy with him as he was only about 12 and still dependent upon him. No one heard from François-Xavier until about 1961 or '62 when it happened that the provincial constabulary arrested him for public drunkenness in Fossambault. Jean-Paul's father secured his release from the jail and tried to help, but Charlevoix refused help and said that all he wanted was oblivion. His father asked after the ex-deacon's adopted son. "I have no son" was the reply. He departed without a goodbye and without giving thanks for the help he was given.

A few months later, it was learned that he had died of liver disease.

I asked Jean-Paul if anything was found out about José Primitivo. He responded that no one ever made the effort to determine his fate, that Jo-Jo (as he was known in Fossambault) was a boy isolated by his avoidance of people, especially those his age, as they were the most apt to tease him, dancing around him and letting out Indian war whoops if they chanced upon him on his way to the library or cinema. In short, no one missed him for they hardly knew him.

I decided to travel to Kitchener, Ontario to continue my investigation. I was hoping that there might be some mention of father or son in local records, police reports, obituaries and the like.

Not sure where to start, I went to the library and discovered that the local newspaper, the *Waterloo Region Record*, bestowed the library with a searchable file of all the articles in its "morgue," dating back to when it was known as *The Kitchener-Waterloo Record*.

I searched for "Joseph-Primitif" and "José Primitivo Charlevoix" and did not find any articles but, in the process I did find one that mentioned

UNIDENTIFIED BODY FOUND IN KITCHENER

The Kitchener police report that the body of a man, estimated to be from 25 to 35 years of age, was found Wednesday morning on Halls Lane, West near Ontario Street, South. The man has not yet been identified.

The police state that, judging from appearances, the dead man is possibly an Indian or a Métis. The cause of death is unknown. There are no signs of foul play. A note was found on the dead man's person with a name and phone number.

The name on the note is Francis Charlevoix. The phone number pertains to the municipality of Sainte-Foy, Quebec. Police unsuccessfully dialed the number and were informed that the number was disconnected last year with no forwarding number registered.

The Waterloo Regional Police Service requests that any persons knowing the identity of the deceased or the whereabouts of Francis Charlevoix contact their office immediately.

The body rests in the Berlin-Waterloo Hospital morgue pending possible identification.

a Francis Charlevoix.

This brief article was dated February 7, 1964. I searched for later articles containing the phrases "body identified" and "man identified" and found only two dating to 1998 and 2007 and referencing a man suffering from Alzheimer's who had wandered away from home in one instance, and a man who had been found drowned in the Grand River in the other.

I went to the police and requested a search of their records. Detective Gordon Urquhart was very accommodating.

He found the file and said that the case had never been solved. No one ever claimed the body and no one inquired after a missing person who would fit the description of the corpse.

Detective Urquhart said there were two significant items found on the body: a penciled note with the name and phone number of Francis Charlevoix and a photograph.

I begged to see the photograph and was shown a square format black and white photo most likely taken with a Brownie or other Kodak camera. It was a photo of a young man in an overcoat and muffler, presumably worn against the cold. The photograph captured him in the act of pulling down the brim of a dark fedora over the right side of his face.

It struck me that the subject of the photograph was too young to be François-Xavier Charlevoix. But could this be José Primitivo?

When I asked this of Detective Urquhart, he laughed and said it was a question that was impossible to answer. He was unamused, however, when I peppered him with more questions.

Did the photograph bear any resemblance to the dead man? Was this photograph published so that someone might identify him by the image in the picture? Were fingerprints found on the photo? What efforts were made to find François-Xavier Charlevoix? Did they contact the Saint-Foy police?

Urquhart seemed irritated, I suspect because my interrogation appeared aimed at uncovering police investigatory incompetence, but he answered me politely, nevertheless.

He said that valid comparisons could not be made between the facial features of the dead man and those of the man in the photo because the face of the person in the photo was partially obscured. Yes, there were fingerprints found on the photo, and they indeed matched those of the dead man, but the photo was in his possession, and it would be natural for his fingerprints to be on it. Since they could not establish that the man in the photo was the dead man, they could come to no conclusions about it. For all the police knew, the person in the photo was Francis Charlevoix or someone else entirely. Calls were placed to the phone number on the scrap of paper, but it had been disconnected some time before. The police in Saint-Foy knew nothing about a Francis Charlevoix.

I informed the detective that the elder Charlevoix died in 1962 or

'63. He wryly remarked that that would explain why the Kitchener police were unable to locate him. He observed that keeping the phone number of a dead man might indicate that the possessor of it was unaware that he was dead.

I asked if I could take a picture of the photograph with my phone camera. Detective Urquhart was hesitant to acquiesce but consented to my request when I made the case that I hoped to publish it in a book and that it might lead to someone identifying the person in the photo.

Urquhart wished me luck and said:

"In spite of the fact that this police department was unable to make a definitive identification between the man in the picture and the dead man, it's obvious to me, and I say this with more than 25 years of service as a forensic detective, that, given all the evidence, they are one and the same. Whether or not this is your José Primitivo...well, maybe. Who's to say?"

As I crossed the bridge from Sarnia into Port Huron, I reflected on the many phantom bridges José Primitivo Charlevoix had been required to cross, the borrowed names that were foisted upon him, the separation from a nation and people that he knew nothing of, save perhaps what his curiosity could gather from books. Did this Hondureño, taken from the crowded winding streets of Tegucigalpa, ever long to see the land of his unhappy birth and abandonment?

We don't know. Certainly, there is no indication of such a desire in his writing.

And what writing! The more I read it the more I am struck by its nagging absurdity that bothers and annoys at the most inopportune times...an absurdity—a unique idiocy—like a small mongrel dog plaguing you, nipping at your heels just as you think you have happened upon something mysterious, majestic, beautiful.

The more I consider the contents of this book, the more I am convinced that the author was—is—a unique artist of the same inexplicable, eccentric genius manifest in Isidore Ducasse and Raymond Roussel.

But as to who he was we have only the most faint of outlines, a man seemingly trying to conceal himself, like the person in the photograph found in the coat of a dead man. He was a man who foresaw that, if not forgotten, he would ultimately be quite unknown.

who am i
who was he
now that i am no longer
now that i am no longer i
now that i have become he
now that there is no witness to what he was
to what he did

Arturo Mantecón
December 2018

JPM

who am i
who was he
now that i am no longer
now that i am no longer i
now that i have become he
now that there is no witness to what he was
to what he did

he was the green grasshopper that loses its vital spring
and he was the green caperberry bereft of powers
helpless[1]

he was a man who would shut his eyes at midday
believing that by the very act of shutting them

---

1. We can confidently infer that this passage refers to Ecclesiastes 12:5 of the Old Testament. The King James version of the OT does not translate the Hebrew הָאֲבִיּוֹנָה literally (caperberry), but rather translates it symbolically as "desire". However, the author, growing up in a religious household in Quebec, probably had access to La Bible de Jérusalem in which the Hebrew word is translated literally. "Quand on redoute la montée et qu'on a des frayeurs en chemin. Et l'amandier est en fleur, et la sauterelle est pesante, et la câpre perd son goût. Tandis que l'homme s'en va vers sa maison d'éternité et les pleureurs tournent déjà dans la rue". ("When going uphill is an ordeal and you are frightened at every step you take- yet the almond tree is in flower and the grasshopper is weighed down and the caper-bush loses its tang; while you are on the way to your everlasting home and the mourners are assembling in the street") The Jews of biblical times believed that the eating of caperberries had an aphrodisiacal effect and, in fact, increased the desire for all things pleasurable. This passage of the bible is usually interpreted as describing the decline of vitality and desire in old age. Whether Charlevoix was referring to himself or to someone else, whether he was describing a loss of vital powers or sense of impending catastrophe or death is, of course, unknown.

he would draw into his presence awful beauties and adorable grotesques
startling mineral vegetable animal chemical freaks
of substance and void
that he could not see
that he could not see because his eyes were shut

he would retreat to distant deserted fields and forests and would shut his eyes
he knew that the fantastic phenomena had come
when he no longer heard the birds
                    the flies
                        the crickets
                            the small mammiferous beasts
                                the chatters
the hums the croaks stilled as they were by the things he summoned

he would shut his eyes on buses trains in crowded eating places and theaters
and would listen for the gasps the screams the babbling as in tongues the
orgasmic moans

then
when the living sounds of remote places returned
when deathly quiet ruled in human spaces
                            he would open his eyes

AND WHO WILL BOTHER

how to tell one from another
another from one
without killing the one
without fate-ing the other
without forking the paths
of the homeward lamb
and the sinful goat
without splintering
the sharp arcs
of the crow
into irrational numbers
it is the mayhem of the word
burning drowning
the soluble body
of the sugar and the salt
the high silk hat
wherein the rabbit disappears
over and over again
to emerge from a sleeve
as a starting bouquet of doves
over and over again
it is to loom the sierpinski carpet
until it lifts up and grazes
the crescent moons
of the inescapable
minarets of baghdad
it is to sweep the dust

of gentile cantors
through those dream
alleys of the souqs
that loll and curl
like ribbons of flesh
like acute angles of smoke
it is to present oneself weeping
and as cock naked
as the humbled jesus
to the cruel gasping laughter
of the godless stars

[MY CLIONA IS]

my cliona is my love
my hatred
my white heaven
my bloodied earth
my glaucous water
my severed veins
my cankered tree
my trampled timothy
my mutilated wasp

cliona waves the wands
of singing birch
as she strides
through the froth and scum
of obeisant seas
casts malachite tourmalines
and oyster seeds
in furrowed surf
and declares
her singular curious devotion
to my destruction
she is the Beatrice
of my miserable purulent eyes
the nomenclator
of my variable feces
and the celebrant
of all my excesses

cliona knifes clean
the black scales
of her sunset dragon
extracting the horrid
rasping grinding worms
from the scuta
cliona makes me bread
out of oak galls
nettles sparrow eggs
and her vinegary piss
cliona has a cat
that walks erect
and carries a fan
and a bamboo cane
i am food for my cliona
the twolegged animal book
of soft lung leather
and onion skin
that she avid eats
with mouth lips
teeth tongue spittle
every weightless page
every black phoenician mark
like the threeeyed iron bull
of the children of ammon
sliding a laughing babe
down its fiery maw[2]

my cliona is my hatred
my tethered wolf
my red sea urchin

my misshapen pearl
my cliona is my love
my bile and gall
my flint and salt
my guilty hands
my nest of yellow ants

2. Here JPC describes himself as a living, edible book to be consumed by his love Cliona. The "black phoenician marks" on the book would seem to refer to the Phoenician origin of the Western alphabet. He apparently views himself as a sacrificial offering to the fearsome Cliona who consumes him as did Moloch, the Phoenician/Ammonite idol, consume the burnt offerings of children.

96857

and i walked the haunted broken streets
of birdravaged gardens and tangling vines
past the deaf and dumb houses
of my past
brick wood stone
to the highest maple boughs
inhabited by firemaned lions that watched me
from the paneless windows and open doors
and the air an invisible tide of urine
and cumin coconut curries
mint and honeysuckle
and of the sweat of women
wood shavings and kneaded mutton
the meagre birds did natter their cruelty
and the lions sang green
and red songs of love
begging me begging me
to draw near
and black squirrels
surged by
in a great flowing tongue to the north
and i was young again
and light of step
and smooth of skin
and mad with wanting
and a hand or trident
parted the boiling clouds

and a voice of crashing iron and gunpowder said
i am the hopeless roar of nothingness
the roar of birth and death
that gives way to the dreadful silence
this is the child I brought into being
with my measureless
whirling brass blades of mighty noise
the child I have kept and comforted
through waking and sleep
with falling waters
meteoric hooves
hums of cicadas
winddriven skittering leaves
endless passing trains
hissing steam
turbines
motored belts and chains
meshing gears
and the fluent breath of sea waves
take him and consume him if you can

i heard the voice
and the lions heard the voice
and the birds heard the voice
and all heard the voice
and i was careless
and light of foot
and pliant of limb
and my skin shone
and i flew over the pavement
and three women drew near to me

women of roses smoke and honey
their hair was the wind
and they said to me
come with us
for winifred would show you her hands
and they took me to a house
and its rampant lions
lowered heads and quieted their desires
then came a room
without walls without roof
and there
on planks of cedar
and blooms and spikes of tuberoses
sat winifred with hands behind her
she was moonfaced and kinkheaded
and her breasts studded and bleeding
with shards of glass
and i knew and she knew
that i wanted
wanted her heat and her hair
and her eyes and her placid ugliness
so that i might finally
so finally might
finally so
as though it were
the end
as though the end
were in her slack and hideous arms

winifred show me your hands
and she put her hands

upon her lap
and clapped them together
and they became one spinning ball
of a black
of the blackest black
and the ball spun until it made a noise
like a monotone
longheld tenors air
and the three women said
ask for something

winifred i want the moon
and her mad spinning hands
became the image of the pocked
and twofaced moon
and it was white and yellow
and red at turns
and full and half and crescent
and i wanted the sun
and her hands became the sun
blinding and burning
and flaring its frenzied desperation
and i wanted a toad
and her hands became
a dark dreadful poison toad
and she presented me a heron
a dog a whale a rose
water fire excrement
all the books in the Bodleian
anger and love and justice
demonfilth

and evil beggaring description
the wax work faces
of my parents
and the naked body of my cliona
she showed me all
but would not show me
nothingness
show me nothingness
and she parted
her hands
and all went silent
she opened her arms
and i entered the arc they described
and she embraced me and opened her mouth
her toothless mouth
from which issued the mephitic odors
of the underworld
and she opened her mouth
her toothless mouth
and i was within her mouth
in darkness
in the blackness
in the horrible silence
where not even god
can hear his thoughts

SIMPLE

all of my bones whistle to the hungering wind
and accost the beamed tariffs of the yawning hull

all of my bones
all of my bones

bid pity from friend from enemy
arrange anger in staggered rows of endless defile
ring with calcitic hammers the white flowering light of the nuclear
sun
are scattered in the flayed subterranean desert
the unhearing desert of nothingness
are strewn in the godly fecality of the ghastly abandoned edens

all of my bones
all of my bones
all of my bones

dust of magic prayers clipped trapped and defanged and arrested
within the phylacteries tangled in the eelcat payots of hideous dead
rabbis
and no amount of davening words shall withdraw my acute eve rib
from the core
of the weeping pachyderm

all of my bones
all of my bones

all of my bones
all of my bones

heavy dumb columnar stones stacking my collapse of arching spine
in paramoudra flints as desolate as the hearts of men
ashes for the springs of corn and the steadfast growing of cultured
fossils
for delicate small white teas

all of my bones
all of my bones

their flesh cut to flaunt my auriferous femur
the longing reliquary blade sheathed in my crooked leg

all of my bones
all of my bones

in ranging lunar lustre
scattered ostophone of perfect fifths

all of my bones
all of my bones

saul of tarsus
skull and vulva
sword and spade
holy bone
sacrosanct thorn

all of my bones

oh mothering yse who suckles the eye of measured time
you mistress of the transparent seas
fashion me a phallus of gold
send me a cankerous woman
an exoskeletal belle to dance the dance of the carrion birds
to dance the dance of hell

all of my bones
all of my bones

QUAND UN TELESCOPE EST HORS DE QUESTION

the man stands upon a milking stool

         three legs and a jutting handle

to get a closer look at the moon
hides behind the chintz
spies

             kaleidoscope in hand

on his neighbours naked virtuous wife frying onions
battered pigs trotters panjumping hissbursting
spattering cottonseed oil coming golden
on the dark dawns of her great falling dugs
cuisine before pain
pain ordinaire
scales the turpentine reaches of the weakest branches
heart bleating like a desperate black lamb
knows the troubles of the impotent pygmies
bee keeping his suit

          not for honey for humming

le bourdonnement of their voicewings invisible to the eye
the eye the sense of
he wishes no one harm merely the manna
the false bottom wine that he knows is all he deserves
caritas
he needs no map just an adequate point of view from the terrazza
vermouth in hand handing her his dreams
humid as open wounds

naked she was naked
you too would look
so much flesh like colliding tumescent darkling clouds
laden with rain and milk and vaginal mucosa
grant him that much
caritas kindly
milk sheep cows
caritas
goats mares
lait le lait dulait
everywhere yanked out
of the concealed murkquartz prism of his birth
capturing afar the horse in question

ABYSMAL BEAUTIFUL FACE

when the eyes finally close
with a great shuddering noise
the clarity begins and we see
                through the translucent viscous
              lids of hair and microscopic parasites
the unending sterility
of everything that has ever touched us
in colour cones and reflected light
                    cartesian optics
                  and stoic physics
                  be damned
for there is never enough to keep us occupied
for there are no concatenations of colliding bodies
that extend the mystery far enough to make us forget
that there is absolutely no reason for us to be here
there is never enough mystery for him to leave us alone
and necessity and nuisance
and secondary sexual characteristics alike
are mere pretensions here
sufficient and efficient cause are paltry fictions
there are other choices
but they are not available on the fourth monday of each month
and guess what day this is
and if you think this is the month of june
you are sadly mistaken

winter is fast coming
and the rapture of the brutal cold wind
rushes up in a spiral to carry you and snail you
in heavens ugly sulphur clouds
like a whirling frozen bleeding rose
hips and waist and thighs and ascorbic acid
and last nights roast beef
cast about in a terrible stinking fleshy slurry
the detritus of the lifeless world
litters the path to my soul
the path that starts in the gaping wound
in the centre of the palm of my hand
and follows the miserable ladder
of my cowardly curving twisted spine
                              and what have my hands done
what could my hands have possibly done to her
that i merit this pain
my hands
my hands that hold the key
the key i want no part of
and i stand at the closed locked door
the accursed key in my hand
and cannot open the door
cannot put the key in the lock
and my entire body frozen
with the fright of an immense love
and a deafening whispering voice roars
that there is no need of a key
that the door is unlocked
but i cannot find the will to push it open
and the door opens on its own

and a beautiful face fills the open doorway
circled and orbited by the phantasms
of benzene rings and carrion flies
and i cannot walk through the door
and the door disappears
and the lintel and threshold vanish
and i cannot walk toward the gigantic abysmal
beautiful face
and the key becomes flesh and bone
the sixth finger of my guilty wounded right hand
and i cannot move cannot move
and then the whispering insistent
incomprehensible voice calling me
calling me calling me
to be swallowed up by that fatal
dark mystery

THE DRAGON AND THE BOAR

a black flowerscaled dragon
winged from the west
toward the east
belching red flame as it flew
in its right hand
a waspscreaming sword
long as a lostforest larch
in its left
a dreadful giant mace
of spikeiron
its tail blunt and stinking
two goldmottled leopard heads
protruded from its breasts
and one
from its distended belly
leopard heads snarlfanging
in desperate spitting rage
from the east
a mad immense boar
covered in bloodseeping warts
shook the earth
with its wildrun treetrunk
ungulate legs
tenfoot tusks whitegleaming
and upcurving

mowing down hardwood forests
and millionsouled cities
in its path
roaring and roaring
until the birds fell dead
from the sky
and granite mountains crumbled
into the valleys
did they crash together
in some stark siberian dream
did the earth quake
did the stars tremble
they did they did they did
and blood flowed
and black scales
and wirethick bristles flew
entrails spilled
leopard heads were severed
white tusks were broken

but this is what you must know
a viola da gamba
makes a beautiful casket
for a dead child

the ewes milk that flows
down the impressed gutters
in loaves of barbarian bread
is best caught
in copper beakers
to be given

in penitence
to the naked orphans

it is in the city
of eternal night
where god
rents his artists studio
from the bearer of light
in which he shapes mud
into uninspired golems
gagged by blank parchment
for it is in the city
of eternal night
that god
in his dementia
has forgotten
his own name

in the city
of eternal night
god is now monstrously
incontinent
and pisses and shits
himself uncontrollably
and in such quantities
as only a hebraic
fiend of stench
and cruelty
can produce

god the uncircumcised

sheds his rags
and dances desperate
through the stony streets
of the city
of eternal night
for god is not dead
but dying
and so spins out
like a drunken joke
his last dance
his last chance
at anything
resembling joy
his dance macabre

give the naked orphans
ewes milk
as an act
of contrition
for your sins

make a beautiful casket
for a dead child

MY LADY OF THE TROLLEYS

je est un autre

i saw her
saw her face conquer
the ambiguous light
her face eggnested
in auburn fox collar
green astrakhan

blue chisping wire sparks
brushed her face
a faint dying violet

grackle feather hair
nutshell frightening
beauty eyes
electrically greyed eyes

stood there
in big toggled
navy coat
genuflecting
swaying
to the docile waves
of king street

with stops and starts
of trolley coach grey
with fits and starts
a sudden epilepsy forward

stood there
eyes
dark underlids
fluorescent pallid
face nested slow tides
her face

eyes jacobean
looking at me
approach me closer come
stand up to me listen
listen closely
ears ears
make of your mouth
a mystery and
hum drone and mewl
ears ears
no intentioned rhetoric
ears ears
no arrows aimed
at the honey maiden
ears ears
tighten lips
speak to me
through your swollen brow
my words shall be the only

assassins
on this wretched trolley
that the underground queen
holds in the palm of her sprouted hand
the wise queen who can touch
motion indivisible itself

attend
me regard
eye in eye
i am about to tell
fortune and misfortune
in the radicals of your hair
the salty poisons of your liver

you are a thistlefine rod
of iron dust
and i will lift you
yearning erect
into the air
like the spiking
morning star

love or else hate
all that finds you
avoid all peace blisses
the exhaled extinctions of fire
for there is nonesuch
nor even in nothing

indifference will not serve

save for ignorance
strive always
for ruthless grandeur
and not for goodness
for goodness was fashioned
and is worn
by the wicked
as a shiny
mesmerising ornament

cling to your cliona
for she will be
the lovely death of you
and that is all
a man can want of a woman
it matters not if you find
yourself a king or a carrier of
dung in this world
for you are and will be a poet

ever heed me
and you
will write poems
that never were

ever you shall think of me
you shall write poems

you shall

they will be poems

poems
informed by measured chaos
singular exemplary
disordering words
flying through canyons
rushing through arroyos
and singing in reverberating
barrancas

poems that will cause
the platonic horse to burst
head haunches hide hair hooves
you will
you will

now close your eyes
to the spattering gore
and open your mouth
to my mantic kiss

and i closed my eyes
and opened my mouth
and i heard the great frantic
murmur of a thousand
whispering animals
and i opened my eyes
as we crossed water
as the trolley coach lurched
and shook
and she vanished
vanished
from my sight

SENSIBILIA

when
my ballistic tongue was new
and my tail had yet
to resort
to autotomy
nothing
was microscopic
and the darkened brambles
of the tinted page
the manycoloured comet jags
of coral
the minute
noble ores
and caracolling lustrin
of the starnumbered sands
were discerned
as though apples
tumbled heads
common herbs
my hands crabbed in the earth
to follow the jewellers eye
and i ate red gems red glass
swallowed wine and blood
for all
that was
sweet was red
and i could see the clouds

of gas
from the upturned stone
i was avid
to inhale
tasting the yellow
the red ant
the millions
of hairpins
fashioned
into an autoerotic
fourdoor ford sedan
redolent
of the pilosebaceous must
of scaling scalps and attarish hair
of maidens wives old dames
black yellow brown copper white red
i ate it ate them
all drank breathed
i could see it
i could see them
vapor
mineral unction
parasite
atomic
liquid cilia
chemic minute
artefact
spicules yeast
my regenerating tail
my ballistic tongue
this was long desperate now

long gone lost
new
no more
it is no more no longer
new tongue tail

CLIONA AND THE GIANT IN THE LAKE

kalokooma the black bear
lamepawed and snoutmangled
came to my love cliona
to complain of a giant
who lived in the big lake
that lies beyond the cold hungry lands
and kalokooma snuffled
and bowed and wept
and begged of my cliona for help
and he did singwail
in resonant tenor throat moan

cliona cliona my barbarous queen
cliona cliona my murderous fiend
i would open my thorax to let out my sorrow
for my beehoney clan and the entirety
of the animals that fill the white woods
and stonerivered wastes

the wapitous moose
the yowling lynx
the damming castors
the whitehead eagles
the moonsinging owl
the wolverine the barbback porcupine

the rooking raven
the quick stripe chipmunk
the coyote and the wolf
and the rancourous badger
have all suffered fearful torment
from the giant that lives 333 fathoms
underwater of our cold deep lake
help us cliona
for he tortures and murders us

for lack of love and soul
he fashioned a net and sweeps the lake
of all our frogs
of all our salamanders
and all of our fish until we starve
or eat eachother dead and alive

and cliona asked

how does this giant
who lives in the lake not drown

and kalokooma answered
that the giant lived in a great cave
beneath the floor of the lake
and that it was told by the great turtle
that the cave was full of air and gentle zephyrs
and had meadows and forests within it
and a small alwaysshining carnelian sun
that hung pierced and suspended
from a lofty stalactite

and cliona said

take me to the lake of the giant
so i may kill him with my sword and hooks

and cliona sat astride the bears back
with her oldwound yellow thighs
and they flew through the air
for her magic
and in 11 heartbeats
were at the shore of the lake
that lies beyond the cold and hungry lands
and cliona walked to the edge of the water
and with her long hemlock flute
played a song to enchant and lure the giant
and the giant
with a frightful spiked club in hand
rose up naked and colossal
from the bottom of the lake
and strode over the black and white rocks
of the marge
and then stopped stockstill and dumbfounded
by the deepsad loonsong of the flute
and cliona dropped her hemlock flute
and before the giant came out of his reverie
threw her grappling hook
at the giants pestiferous crotch
and it caught in the inguinals near his cock
and she climbed up faster than a spider on her silk
and took out her demonkilling sword
and severed the giants cock

which fell with an earthshaking crash
and the giant came to full and awful awareness
as he bled and bled in a cascade of gore
that flowed from the stump of his loss
and cliona reached up with her shining sword
and gashed the giants abdomen
and with another longhandled hook
pulled out the giants entrails
and his guts fell out so fast
that they overwhelmed cliona
and they fell on her and pulled on her
and she tumbled entangled to the bloody ground
as the giant fell backward
with head and shoulders landing in the prussic lake
making an immense upward uproar
of white water and foam

and kalokooma summoned all the animals
out of the white woods
and they all dug and clawed and tore
at the steaming guts of the giant
until they reached cliona
who emerged gleaming and expelling
vapours of blood and pus
from her matchless skin and coarseworming hair

bring me dead leaves twigs and branches and flint
ordered cliona

and we will feast

and the animals brought kindling and flint
and soon the giants cock
was roasting over the fire
and the giants cock fed many as it was 12 feet long
and since the square root of any giant is his cock
it can be calculated well that the giant was 144 feet tall
and when 100 of the animals had had their fill of roasted cock
cliona spied that the hogsized crablice
that had lived and thrived
in the black hairfilth of the giants crotch
        were jumping in escape
and cliona overtook 51 of them
and sliced off their heads and put them in the fire
and fed many more of the souls
of the white woods
another 27 lice
she caught and kept in cages
and in a few days had tamed them
and taught the animals to milk them like goats
but it was blood that the crablice gave
and not milk
and the blood they dried
and shaped into cubic cakes
and those cakes
and the rotting flesh of the dead giant
fed many for many and all days
until the end of days
and the lice bred and many of the hatched nymphs
in singlefile followed cliona home
as she walked back through the cold hungry lands
and cliona foreverafter refused to fly

CLIONA WANTED AN EGG

cliona wanted an egg
an egg within an egg
an egg of iron
an egg of nickel
an egg one million
five hundred twentyeight thousand
four hundred and eighty feet
and five inches
across
an egg of embryonic
mercaptan yolk
that she would mark
for fascinating the
virulent
vapourdriven serpents
that constant pursue
her hard corn heels
an egg to charm
the satellite bracelets
that orbit her scabbed wrists
as orthorhombic moons

bring me an egg
the command

get me the nickel and iron
heart of a wanderer
a subtle
andhakaradical thunderstone
the colliding alloy
of planetesimals
cowl your head
with a giant lily bell
fetch my earless
widmanstatten cup
find my tapping spoon
of siderous ores
bridging the widest waters

build your flying bark
with blooddark quebracho
and colossal loadstone

and with levitating
adamant rocks
pitch and toss by degrees
all the way
to the sun's mirror
crack its calcium
carbonate shell
with the gaveled handle
of my farreaching
spoon
dig dig dig
in the pockfaced
gibbous moon

and return to beula
to our cobalt lake
in the red mapled forest

and I did as I was told
I did as I was
told and did
as I was
told I did
as I was told
and I did
I was told and I did
as
I cowled and fetched
I found and did build

Pitched and tossed
I cracked
I did dig I dug and I dug
through basalts
of olivine
and prismatic crystals
through to the
sulphurical
ferrous yolk
lowered my flying ship
to mesmerize
the innocent mind
of the egg within
the egg
pulled it out with

a length of my clionas
braided hair
and sank
head cowled
in the bell
of a preposterous
lily
sank below and against
the tides of regret
back to the earth
back to beula
back to the cobalt lake
in the red mapled forest
to deliver
black and ponderous
spinning redundant
in the erratic generation
of heretofore unknown
transcendental numbers
numbers of aloe
opoponax
dutchmans pipe
balms of giliad
grapes of goat dung
to salve
the calcaneus skin
subject to the mortal
yet welcome bites
of the familiar
virulent
vapourdriven serpents

that constant pursue
the hard corn heels
of my cliona

[MY CLIONA DESCENDED]

my cliona descended
and lifted the glaucous
tides as she came she
did not laugh she did not
weep but her face was
ghastly wet
blood and grease

what have you done
with my words above
the din of the hooves
have you followed the nails
of my wisdom my hair
have you eaten the crumbs
of my fear open
the book
for my pharmacology
is gone and the light
of its leaves
has dried dried
the disenchantments
the liver the pluck
and gall the beasts
of the sudden cure
the watching ghosts
of the holy sickness
the sacred death of my

loves you loves
loves you love
until we can coil
and moulder together
in our skins
take me and open
my ribs and issue
that genderless creature
we have spoken of for days
and dreamed of for nights
come down with me rise
up with me so
that we may never be alone again

[HAMMURABI CAME TO ME]

hammurabi came to me
       with the morning star
           in the skittering light
              of the sinning moon
    his plaited beard
    a forbidding brass
       his eyes plucked out
       from his flaming head
         his firelocked head
         mitred and circled
by galanning birds
of boolbool song

oh my blind hammurabi

a freshly severed
glistening cock
of a googalana bull
a cradled babe
in his terrible arms

cock of a thundering
rain bull
a bloody
yet yearning

stele black rampant
cut and toothed
with the lex talionis
of codified revenge

oh my hammurabi

tremble limbs lurid
did deplorably moan

      mooshoossoo
      the alacranical dragon
      has betrayed me
      to follow the taloned stride
      of she
      who would have me dead
      for scribing
      her underground decrees

      lilith
      owlwinged queen
      of the sickening nightwinds

and the law giver
said to me

      defend me my life
      and compound beguiling
      poison
      for the red splendor
      serpent

feed mooshoossoo
sodom apples
cakes of blue stone
wine of mandrake
and hundredleg venom
kill the bloodscaled beast
and soften the dark maid
with honouring sacrifice
and fearful worship

and hammurabi hid himself
within the chambered secrets
of the walls of babylon
with phallic legislation
malleable clay
and golden stylus

and i filled many delights
with evil powders
heavy metals
witching potions
and pharmaceutical death

and mooshoossoo drank
ate and took into lungs
and writhed bellowing
into nettled wilderness
of jackal and vulture
to knead a hollow
in the blasted dust
and heave rattle die

then with magic
hammurabigiven purses
of dumbfounding
minas and talents
i bought at the markets
the distinct crops
of thirtysix green fields
fivethousand lilacbreasted rollers
fivehundred hoopoes
onethousand babblers and beeeaters
gazelles horses ducks
geese exalted doves
and the fat tails
rump and fat
and butterbread marrow
of sixhundred and sixtysix
fattail lambs

all this i drove
in thirtysix four oxen
thunderwood carts
down to the blue river
where the hooloopu stands
hollow willow of knowing
hollow cottonwood of wedding
downy bed of copulation
stolen from the sexcrazed inanna
by cunning lilith
her lionhead flood bird
and her wise noxious snake

and i placed the offerings
on her altar of exile
murderous sea
heaventime and wilderness
i fanned the smoke of vetivert
allspice nutmeg and calamus
and sang praise
at the corners of the stone

her bird and snake
took in the abject smoke
but lilith was vile
in anger and rebuke

      i will fly from my tree
      with the sinning moon
      with beak and claw
      to break your bones
      and i will litter your ribs
      so i may swallow your heart
      i will find the thief
      who stole my laws
      i will shred his flesh
      for vulture and dog
      i will take his bullcock
      to my chambered willow
      and 40 days ride it
      till his scratchings
      are scalded
      by the acids of my venery

and i fled from there
from sinning moon
from the angered wings
of lilith shining
shining with rage and bile
i fled running
i fled hopeless
of hiding
i fled running
begging to the sky
of marduk
to summon crows
to pursue lilith to the sea

and crows in amazements
of black clouds
pursued lilith to the sea
where the ninth wave
swept her down
and into the undersea
mountain
where glistening tiamat
welcomed her
where she found
her lost serpent
children
her books of science
and incantation
where happy
she forgot me
and the stolen laws
of my blind hammurabi

THE ELECTRIC CAR

the electric car
rattled and shook
through the slate
and lead streets
past the huge
barescuffed
hands and digits of trees
passing the end of the line
breaking
from the overhead cables
of sagging sex and fired ozone
lifting
from the pigsquealing
tracks
into the lead and slate
sky toward the farther
pole
where the demiurges of chance
rule in wondrous treachery

it descended
all eiderdown
onto a meadow
of piebald mice
dwarf birds of paradise
landloping fish

i tug the cord
ring the bell
the conductor opens
the brief accordion
and i step
into the red beeclover
mascarene mallows
and mannagrass

i a boy of ten years
bluebilled cap
shirt redgreen windowpane
step 20 steps
and the yellow
shecat
rings in ears
ring in nose
saunters out
of bulrushes bended
questioning
tail oubaste tamita

i follow to answer
follow toward
the hermetic temple
of the three times
magnificent
moonbeaked bird
the bird of the rushes
and the water lilies
who would plant

within my small body
the sharp germ of making
                the greasy praxis
                of the mechanics
                of the gods
who would teach me
the fateful sadness
of heaven goats
bulls and fish
who would give me over
to the betrayal
of glass to gems
of dross to gold

BLACK MOUNTAIN

quantity is everything
not enough
twomuch

pay attention
listen carefully

quantity is everything
recipes for being
meals for kali
the filth
the blood of nothingness
the blind measure
of the abyss
bon chat
bon rat reductions
a night without stars
the ratgnawed holes
of the black bowl
finally
dammed

pay attention
31 oxen
22 vacated cows
of withered udder
49 tons of all purpose

flowers
76 lifesized marzipan
boars
        all marzipan is
        lifesized
big trumpets
consumed difficulty
67 degrees
of difficulty

listen carefully
the contents of pustules
etiology inconsequential
erupting the inner thighs
of inkstained women
literary
in a ratio
three to one
of the above

fold   seethe   shock
then
733 dreamyeyed
poetasters
again
517 femur bones
13 kirtled kingbeards
58 murexdyed phoenician
sailors
8664 and a half
irrational numbers

pay attention
pay
attention

stiraddandor
subtract
85 mice
31 pounds
of flax and hemp
4 impure thoughts
94 paternosters
no nines no nines
death
burn it all
flames
blueredyellowwhite
burn all
until all light swallowed
and the rebeginning
black
time
black time
time of stone without
the accursed dividing
of day
damn the eyes
damn the tongue
suffer empty
the fulfillment
all wishes denied
hopes annihilated dreams

destroyed complete
fulfillment
of desperation
attend horrid silence
time

THE TOAD

1

500 years ago
when green branches and leaves
grew out of my head
and my cock was a red carnation
i searched for the godhead
as one would a vile vagrant dog
and i searched through dark forests
with saffron monks
deserts with a white barefoot nun

dancing mountains
and timeless torrents
i crossed
until i came to a barren plain
through which stretched
the looming wall
of the collision of opposites
the wall of mutual denial
upon which many saints
and magic kings
and gymnosophists
had pissed in their ignorance

and i walked along the wall

for an evil number of days
and saw nothing but
ponderous stones
and the festering bodies
of many lambs and donkeys
and oxen and men dead
from despair

and at last i saw
old nikola
the cardinal nix
emerge
from the earth
like a great spineless worm
and he approached me
naked as a sword blade
and speaking he said

one two three four ten
all that roils on the face
of the earth and in the heavens
meets at this wall
this wall that surrounds
and keeps contained
the beastly blinding black fire
of the impossible infinity of worlds
the infinity of suns and moons
the infinity of poetic voids
and all that we know
and love and despise
coincides here black and white

hot and cold beauty and ugliness
love and hate sanity and insanity
the many and the one
and all things
in hard shining opposition
crash together to form
this terrible wall that shields us
from the horrible absolute
on the other side

i tell you shun
the conquering silence
and give up your search
for there is no god but nothingness
and horrid silence
but do not despair
for there is another you should seek
go on your way toward the night
one two three four ten

and i walked to the west
and again i thirsted
thirsted not for knowledge
nor ignorance nor god nor demon
but for water simple
and far off i saw
what i took for a fata morgana
but thought it better to drink
of an illusion than to have nothing
to drink at all
and so walked toward the mirage

expecting it to vanish
and found
it was a placid blue pool

and near the waters edge
i saw at the dark margins
of the thick gathering weeds

                    a poison toad
                    beckoning to me
            with eyes empty and alldevouring

2

i have lived in this fearful land
for so many ages
slandered by the faithful
in their squat stone churches
and i have been so quietly cursed
for so long
that i have committed murder
with knife with club
with acid and fire
simply to feel
sufficiently worthy
of the whispers

                    into the ragged ears
                    of my neighbour
that i am a flesheating rat
and a thief of souls
and i have been silent

speaking to no man or woman
and crossing words whistles
and groans with animals only

and it has been
some difficult number of days
since a fugitive yellow bird alit
upon my shoulder and wept
and wept complaining
that he could not bring himself
to sing anymore
that he wanted to sing thoughtlessly
and without cause
as he once did
when he was a caged captive

and he could not sing anymore
now that he was free
and lived on the crumbs and scraps
he could wrest away
from the street sparrows
that plagued him
                        all short lives and
                        fastbeating hearts
and he hated them but envied the crow
that so easily could sing his songs
of crushed bones and constricted love

why do you tell me these things yellow bird

because you like me are unable

to sing through the hatred
that chokes your gorge with bile
and so i hate my limitless wings
and the unsummoned wind
and you hate that others
see you for what you are not
all the while wanting to be
that insult to their god
that they take you to be

so you a yellow bird
come for sympathy
from a willfully mute
and dirtwretched man
already stained
with the redviolet ochre
of the caverns shallow grave
for i have lived in this fearful land
for so many ages
that my countless forgotten deaths
have become the shadows
of trees and vanquished springs
and the mineral flowers
of decay
so i can give you no comfort
nor any harsh words of a scold
i can but give you a parting octave
of tightpressed lips
and generous crimes

and the yellow bird took his leave

and i was alone for 5 days of trouble
until i saw at the dark margins
of the thick gathering weeds

                      a poison toad
                  beckoning to me
           with eyes empty and alldevouring

3

i set out
to make a lair
for my cliona
set out to hollow
erect and furnish
a mousery hole
a rabbit warren
dug into the earth
deep deep
and vast spread
a stone and twig thatched
and cakemud wattled
fortress castle
a monackus nonackus
hermetical tower sky high
and grandly impositional
but invisible to naked eyes
and diamond hard

a lair a hold a keep
a matrix a nestdwelling

a memorious lodge
a residing house
for her vapourous spirit
a place to hide in
run to sleep in
sew in rend in
burn in consume in
and for to make and undo
and for to kill and kiss
and for to loudly shit
out of scarcity
and out of plenty

and when i was done
in my digging and weaving
and daubing and joining
and building and concealing
my cliona said

let our domus have no thing
no good
no fixed and fast
no chair no bed
no table no mat
no straw
bring me only stones
big and small on which
to throw ourselves
and pound and grind
our coarsegrit flour

and i brought her ponderous rocks
for her to drape
her crooked shanks upon
and stones fit for killing
the adulterous
and pebbles chips and flakes
to tool and formulate
our daily needs

and my cliona my lame cliona
my springheeled cliona
my bilious choleric squinting
warty molespotted longeared
tufthaired hideous cliona
declared that all
was to her satisfaction
and bade me find three naga sadhus
and fetch them to her
that she might fuck them
until nothing be left of them
but ash and sandalwood smoke

and i left her for that search
and ran in the direction
of fossambault
ran for 5 days and then slowed
my steps and stopped near the lac

where i saw at the dark margins
of the thick gathering weeds

a poison toad
beckoning to me
with eyes empty and alldevouring

4

i was thirsty
i was thirsty
with a thirst
that i thought was unquenchable
i was thirsty with a thirst
for water sweet salty cold hot tepid
dirty clear mineral oleaginous rainborn
slow childish streaming
goat panicked rushdriving river
brown god river
lakes of beulah land
darkest blue
green swarming ponds
their diseases
rising up in the sunlight

i was thirsty
thirsty even for cold metals
steel swords and rings of gold
brass monkeys silver plate
and copper coins
that i would lap up
and swallow
down my smooth

pewtersided throat

i was thirsty
thirsty for vice and virtue
thirsty for the graces
for the muses
for the furies for the fates

i was thirsty
and thirsted for flesh
and blood and bone
and the souls
of all unborn delights

i was thirsty for devils
demons maleficent angels
oottookoos rakshasas
and tzitzimimeh

i was thirsty
and thirsted for truth
and falsehood alike
for rocks and phantasms
heaped into great misfortunes

i was thirsty
and thirsted with a lust
and a desiccated tongue
for knowledge
for knowledge of all good
knowledge of all evil

and i bit my thumb
in search of the wet
leaping salmon of the water
and wandered past the dry
dead well of wisdom

until i saw at the dark margins
of the thick gathering weeds
a poison toad
beckoning to me
with eyes empty and alldevouring

5

i tired of my loneliness
and so i became a hermit
i wearied of my sadness
and so i wept and wept for no thing
and i despaired of my own words
and sealed my lips with mud
and i despaired of the words of others
and the wax of my ears increased
until i was deafened

and two lit candles
emerged from my head
and books convulsed and died
as soon as i took them up
and they rotted away and stank

like so many fetid blankeyed fish

and the sun saddened me
and i waited each evening
for its descent below
the limit of the hopeless desert

and the moon mirrored my strangled heart
and i prayed to the void
to blacken the moon

and i tired of touching the rocks
the sand the waters
my head my face my cock
and my hands lost their sensible powers
and i tired of wandering
and my legs lost all feeling
and collapsed under me
and all expectation saddened me
and my yearning
for the recuperation
of all that had saddened me
made me sadder still

and i wanted to put an end to it
and put an end to my miserable self
and that wanting made me happy at last
and i hunched myself forward
on my bleeding elbows
to find some fire some deep cloacal hole
some unfathomed cliff

and i crept and dragged my detestable body
until in the middle distance i saw
at the dark margins
of the thick gathering weeds
a poison toad beckoning to me
with eyes empty and alldevouring

6

i am an ecstatic fullness
of wanting
for the liquid luxury
of women
for the leeches
of their vaginal lips
for the hardened fascist sulphur
of their heads and hands
and calloused feet

i fly out of my selfsame soul
for sugar and oil
for the tallow of the kine
for boiled beaks and infant bones
in a world without end
and i ever crave a purse
of radishes
rouges et noirs
i desire the milk fingers
of the capricious teat

and fishroe and sowbellies
and sauce of salt and skin
and vinegar and smear

i would pour me the sinews
of the 400 rabbits
grape and tuber
and fruit and sap
and durable grains
for i want to down it all
to leave all language behind
in the acrid vomit
of long long snakes
the forgetful poisons
of annulment
of abandon

and so i blunder
luxuriant of sex and tongue
blind and avid
to devour the rare breasts
of howling anchorite women
i strike with club and flute
and pig bladder
the simpering white clown
of forbearance
i nail the harp
for sleeping smoke
the pipe dreams
of listing cock of full throat
and glutting belly

and i wanted so
i so wanted
i wanted
so
that i took a count of boards
to the insect meadow
to make my table
to burden with limbs and joints
with cellophane eel
and naked bird
with shells and pluck
with heads and tails
with wine and ferment
with the fetid pastes and game
of cave and rafter
with the honeyed feminine
and deathlonging

and i piled and heaped
all of it high
and climbed atop the flesh
and fantastic devotions
to see if i could mark the abyss

and in the middle distance i saw
at the dark margins of the thick gathering weeds
a poison toad beckoning to me
with eyes empty and alldevouring

7

it happened one day
that my kidneys burst
giving out a forceful shower
of urine and blood
and two mineral red
sparkle infants emerged
from my sides
and they were
twin mercuric sulfide babes
who told me
with their crystal mouths
that i could find
unmeasurable wealth
by taking
the unbending way east
to the deathless mother of the road
who with invincible needles
had sewn together in a great thread
many miles
of round and square coins
of copper silver and gold

and my red babies led me
through the thorny thickets where
the straight and narrow commenced
and i walked it
through the brambles
through forests

over meadows
and over wasted spaces
and over flooded lands
and over mountains
and under mountains
and through the bouldered misery
of steepsided valleys

and at last i came upon
a woman with eight arms
seated on an immense
heavy teated sow

and in one hand she held the sun
and in another hand
she held the moon
and in her third hand
a hangmans noose
and the fourth held
a fearsome curving razor
and the fifth
a curious ivory needle
with a length of thread
and in her sixth
a white orchid
as big as a mans head
and her two remaining hands
she placed before her
held together palm to palm
in a beggars supplication

and three faces she had
and the forward one was black
and beautiful beyond understanding
and the others faced to left and right
and the left was the face
of a joyful white mummer
and the right was the face
of a longsnouted swine

and i said
to the mother of the road

what would you have of me
and the mother of the road said

i would have you drink the milk
of my ladle and my plow
the milk
of the fat ponderous sow
that is my throne
so that more red children
may grow inside you

and i got down
on hands and knees
and sucked at the sow
until i could drink no more
until the milk fell from my chin
to the ground
and the mother of the road said

follow me

and i followed her
and we came to a clearing
in the woods
and an immense stove
of iron and nickel
fell slowly from clouds
and landed like a feather
on a blanket of silk
and the mother of the road said

take lead and mercury
and crystals of arsenic
and roast them with orris root
and calamus and mandrake
roast them
until all turns to red stones
then cut into your bowels
with my razor and place
the cinnabar within you

and i did as she asked
and roasted lead
and mercury and arsenic
and i cut myself open
with her fearsome razor
and stuffed my entrails
with red stones
and my wound
closed in an instant

and she rode ahead of me
five rods
and halted her sow
and the mother of the road
handed me the end
of a golden thread
and she said to me

follow it and haul it in hand
over hand and you will be
the richest man on earth

and i did so
and went many miles
and many days
and the thread
passed through countless
round and square coins
and with each i picked up
the wound in my body
opened and the gaping wound
swallowed the coin
before closing up once more
and this happened again and again
with every copper with every silver
with every gold coin

and ravens and magpies
alighted in my path
to tempt me
with pearls in their beaks

and diamonds in their talons
to tempt me to drop the thread
but i remained true to my word
to the mother of the road
and true to my deeper avarice
until at last
there were unknown weights
of coins in my body
yet i felt light and unburdened
and it seemed to me
that my soul left my body
and left the straight and narrow road
of fortune
and my soul hovered
above a rushing stream
where a great antlered stag
had stopped to drink
and the stag with noble head
motioned to my bodyless soul
to follow the river to its source
and my animal force followed the river
until it dwindled into five small streams

and then there
in the middle distance i saw
at the dark margins
of the thick gathering weeds
a poison toad beckoning to me
with eyes empty and alldevouring

8

i punted my raft of hemlock
down la riviere de la betise
to the lighthouse
of the old french stronghold
that looks at the cold big lake
and i walked the breakwater
through crashing waves
and up the snailing steps
to the lanthorn to gaze
at the soulless anger
and to dream of lead to gold
and to dream of dung to roses
transubstantiated between
the freak teeth
of a silent machine

for my cliona had told me
to go and invent things
for the sole sake of invention
to shape
                              out of the accidental wind
the oil the chords
the cogs the chains
the rods and the wheels
of the fetus of the nonesuch

and i hunkered
below the slow dervish

lantern of lightning
and set to dreaming and making
and sine minibus
i made a machine of soapstone
tallow bird wings
and catalpa wood
a machine with a mouth
and fleshy purple lips
that spat out rubies
of bloodseed
that germed and brought forth
the verbal heads of danton
and holy john the baptizer
singing loudly and in counterpoint
     of bread and meat and blades
     and locusts and audacity
     and the seven doors of hell
and i set to dreaming and making
and sine oculis
i made a machine of worm fibres
powdered glass
menstrual blood
and rare earth magnets

a machine
with a sulfurdevil
stinking anus
and it shat and ejected
an aircraft
an immaculate
weightless vegetable soul

that i mounted and flew
north to the dunes
of the dead and buried bear

and i flew crashing into the sands
and regaining my drunken feet
i trod onward

and in the middle distance i saw
at the dark margins
of the thick gathering weeds
a poison toad beckoning to me
with eyes empty and alldevouring

9

and the poison toad spoke
and i listened

and the toad said

come near to me come
into the bullrushes and get on your belly
so that your ear will be at my mouth
the better for you to hear me
the better for you to understand me

and i did as the toad wanted
and the toads eyes awakened and fixed me
with a look the most beautiful i had ever seen

a regard allconsuming that only an angel
                    cast out from the highest skies
could possess

and the toad spoke and i did not speak
                    for i had no need to speak

and the poison toad spoke softly and said

i am the dark ox who grazed on the grasses of heaven
i am the light bearing buffo who battles against the great blind fool
that petty envysickened
dabbler and shaper of mud
that man worships on his knees
                    i crawled from the black vulva
                    of the murderous mother of nothingness
i am the mystery of the white lily
i am the cannibal star that will swallow the sun

and then the toads voice turned to a ground trembling croak
and the toad swelled and doubled in size
and the toad did bellow like a nightcalling lion

and said

i know that you want to lick my soulawakening skin
you want to take my bossy tumoured head into your mouth
to suck on it like a teat
to suck on it like a cock
                    you want to climb the tree of the monad
                    you want to create a god or daimon within you

                    with my venomous science
but before i permit this
before i give you the treasure you covet
you must see to it that i have blood
for i desire the blood of men and women

and the toad commanded and said

get up and turn to the setting sun
and walk 500 paces
yes over there
                    do you see do you see the tall standing rock
                    the menhir of the black heralds
approach it and climb it
for at the top of the stone
you will find a great bell and hammer
                    strike the bell with the hammer
and my hermaphroditic children
who are the numbers and awful noises
of the powerful watchers
will fall upon the men and women of this ignorant world
and will slash throats and will cut wrists
and strike off heads and will set blood to coursing its way to me
in an undeniable red emanation

and i hurried toward the stone
fearful now and regretting having wanted
to know the terrible fright of the hidden

and i reached the menhir of opaline flint
and scaled its sides to the top

where i found the heavy hammer
and the immense bell
suspended from a brass frame and yoke

and i struck the bell
and a sound like the long sustained
roaring of an iron bull filled the air

and as the din of the bell faded
another sound came to my ears
as a distant confused noise
of a vast host of voices
and the murmur grew louder and louder
and i came to understand that the noise
was the rushing progress
                              of a great fluid being
and the trees in the distance began to shake and sway
as if buffeted by a herd of elephants

and out of the forest and into the clearing
came a river of blood
                              a thunderous raging flood
one hundred metres across
that frothed and foamed
as it sped toward the tall upright rock

and i climbed to the top of the bell
                              and clung to its crown
with all the fear that i had
and the river of red blood collided with
                              the menhir of the black messengers

and rushed around it
and swept halfway up its sides
spattering me with hot clotted gore

and the blood sped toward the toad
the toad now swollen to gigantic size
the toad with its mouth gaping
the toad with its obscene tongue extended 20 metres
its tongue twitching and jerking upward in hideous excitement

and the river of blood
                    the immense red snake
leapt up off the ground and surged
into the toads yawning mouth and down its throat

and the river of blood kept coming
and the toad kept increasing in body
and was now as towering and as broad
as a toltec temple

and the river of blood
kept flowing into the toads mouth

                    and the toad grew as big as a mountain
                    and the toads head touched the clouds
and as the last drop of the river of blood
went skyward to the mouth of the toad
all went silent
not a sound was to be heard

and of a sudden

the toad exploded
the toad exploded
noiselessly
and the earth was still
and its creatures all were mute
as fragments of the toad blasted out
to the four directions and to every point between them

and where the pieces of the toads skin
and bones and entrails fell to earth
and where every drop of blood
within the toad fell
there sprang up countless other toads
and impossible flowers and forests
and newborn hills and lakes
and strange birds and teeming
neverbeforeseen insects
and peaceful beasts and killing beasts

and particles of the toads brain and liver
and black bile
landed on my face
landed in my eyes
and a great senseless curtain was drawn and lifted
and all that was before me an instant ago was gone

and there now before me was my cliona
cliona my stinging goad
cliona my harsh love
cliona my merciful nemesis
holding in one hand her long devilsharp sword

and in the other a balance
and on one side of the balance
                        my wild pulse heart
and on the other
                        the staring monstrous
                        bloody head of god

WHAT CLIONA DID WITH THE HEAD OF GOD

when cliona rent a gash
in the heavy magic
of the painted curtain
she found the lionheaded
reptilian
she found the piddler
the dabbler the vile
ignorant tinkering
craftsman
squatting amongst his brushes
chisels hammers knives
and sticks
shaping
from his own foul dung
the men and weeds and moons
and dogs and spiders
of his presumption
and when the foolish
journeyman
saw cliona
he out of desperate spite
clouted the men and women
of dung with his fist of quake

his fist of fire and flood
and he throttled and
shook his cock and misted
his thin yellow sperm
over the come to life
effigies
of babes and children
poxing them
with weeping sores
sickness and death
all out of spite
all out of small
capricious envy

ignorant impostor
screamed cliona
as she raised
her devil sharp sword
above her right shoulder
and brought the bright
droning blade down to cut off the head
of the scourge of men
and she picked up
the openmouthed head
by its long matted mane
and with another stroke
brought down
the pretty rags
of illusion
and stood before me
suspended

on the blank
pointless geometry
of the noumenal

and she said

we will go you and i
we will quick march
together for 6 months
we will giantstride
800000 miles
with each eyeblink speed
of step
for six months
until we are beyond all
memory of dust gas
and difference
until we are at the edge
of the light
and there we will find
a black stonewalled well
8 miles square
8 miles deep
filled complete
with finest wool
of snow fallen lambs
there we will call
the sparrow of the monad
to carry the wool away
one strand at a time
at intervals

of one hundred years

and when the little bird
has at last flown off
with the last
filament of wool
we will burn the vile
head of wisdoms bastard
in the fire of the fullness
and one will be irrationally
divided by zero
and we will commence
to sleep to dream
our own infinity of planets
and stars and wilderness and waters
and unending friends and lovers
out of space
out of time

READING GUIDE

Theme: **Detective Fiction**

The Shadow of the Wind, by Carlos Ruiz Zafón*, involves a man's decades-long search for the life story of Julián Carax, a disappeared and presumably dead author who leaves behind only his book (The Shadow of the Wind) and his name. In much the same way Before the Dark Comes involves an investigation into the life of Jose Primitivo Charlevoix.

In *The Shadow of the Wind*, the searcher is named Daniel Sempere, and as a young boy he is taken by his bookseller father to a secret labyrinthine library in Barcelona called The Cemetery of Forgotten Books. There he picks out a book whose contents and whose author are to haunt him for life.

Representative Work
- *Refer to the Editor's Note for discussion of this prompt*

Prompt(s):

- In what way does the search for the identity of José Primitivo Charlevoix differ from the search for the identity of Julián Carax?
- In which ways are they similar to the detective work put to use to identify Julián Carax in *The Shadow of the Wind*?

---

* Carlos Ruiz Zafón. The Shadow of the Wind. The Penguin Press, 2004.

Theme: **The Absurd/Surreal**

In *Before the Dark Comes*, the surreal, the absurd, grotesqueries, and the carnivalesque are all to be found. Although these categories often intersect or overlap, surrealism stresses the weird images of the unconscious realm, absurdist literature asserts the irrationality and chaos of the real world, grotesque literature fixates on the ugly and repulsive, carnivalesque in literature subverts literary norms through humor and abundant disorder.

Representative Work

- "96857"
- "quand un telescope est hors de question"
- "the dragon and the boar"
- "black mountain"

Prompt(s):

- Which of these four categories of the surreal, the absurd, the grotesque and the carnivalesque predominates in Before the Dark Comes?
- Which of these four categories is of least significance?

Theme: **Unconventional feminine beauty / Male subservience to female strength**

Cliona is a heroine of a horrifying beauty according to Jose Primitivo Charlevoix. Beauty and horror are two things that are not normally associated with each other. Are they contradictory? Can there be women who are both horrifying and beautiful? Or can they have a beauty that is horrifying? Can beauty itself be horrifying? José Primitivo swears that he loves Cliona and yet he describes her as fearsome as well as fearless. He describes himself as Cliona's food. He slavishly follows her every command and sings of her murderous ferocity.

Representative Work
- "cliona and the giant in the lake"
- "my cliona descended"
- "[my cliona is]"
- "The toad" (see section 3)

Prompt(s):

- Is José Primitivo in love with her female strength or does he simply fear Cliona?

ACKNOWLEDGMENTS

My thanks to Christina, my wife, without whose support this book could not have been produced.

And my gratitude to J. K. Fowler, Michaela Mullin, Noelia Cerna (my editor) throughout the pre-publication process; and others of Nomadic Press.

Arturo Mantecón

Arturo Mantecón is a poet and literary translator, whose poems have appeared in various reviews and anthologies. His books of translation include three volumes of the collected works of Leopoldo María Panero and selected works by Francisco Ferrer Lerín and Mario Santiago Papasquiaro.

COVER MISSIVE

On "Houston Toad"
by Lisa Studier

"Houston Toad" is a woodcut print created as part of a series of woodcut portraits depicting endangered reptiles and amphibians. The Houston Toad (Anaxyrus houstonensis) is an endangered amphibian endemic to Texas. It lives in pine and oak woodlands and savanna and is most threatened by habitat loss, pesticides, and drought. Only a few thousand remain.

OTHER WAYS TO SUPPORT NOMADIC PRESS' WRITERS

In 2020, two funds geared specifically toward supporting our writers were created: the **Nomadic Press Black Writers Fund** and the **Nomadic Press Emergency Fund**.

The former is a forever fund that puts money directly into the pockets of our Black writers. The latter provides dignity-centered emergency grants to any of our writers in need.

Please consider supporting these funds. You can also more generally support Nomadic Press by donating to our general fund via nomadicpress.org/donate and by continuing to buy our books. As always, thank you for your support!

Scan below for more information and/or to donate.
You can also donate at nomadicpress.org/store.